ISBN 978-1-338-19558-3

12 11 10 9 8 7 6   18 19 20 21 22

Printed in the U.S.A.   .   40

First Scholastic printing, April 2017

Book design by Lucy Ruth Cummins
The text for this book is set in Typewrither.
The illustrations for this book are rendered in pencil and watercolor, and assembled digitally.

IT CAME IN THE MAIL

Ben Clanton

SCHOLASTIC INC.

Liam loved to get mail.

Too bad he never got any.

He checked ~~daily~~

 ~~hourly~~

every few seconds,
but found . . .

. . . diddly-squat.

But then, on a day much like any other,
an idea struck Liam.

If he sent some mail,
then maybe he'd get some in return.

Not sure who to send something to,
Liam sent a letter to his mailbox.

Dear Mailbox,

I would like to get something in the mail. Something BIG! PLEASE!

Love,
Liam

As soon as Liam put the letter in,
the mailbox began to shake.
It made all sorts of strange sounds.

KRINK

When Liam looked inside,
he was met by a blast of fire.
A dragon had come in the mail!

And it was for Liam.

Liam loved the dragon.
But he couldn't wait to see what
he might get next!

Dear Mailbox,

Thank you for the
fire-breathing dragon.
It is just what I
always wanted.
Can you send me more
stuff? PLEASE!
          Love,
                Liam
P.S. You are the best
mailbox ever!

Soon the mailbox was spitting
out all sorts of things.
Pickles! Pigs! A whale with wings!
A trombone! A triceratops bone!
Even a funny bone!

Liam liked it all!
He liked it all so much
that he wanted even more.

Oodles and oodles of mail
flooded out of the mailbox.

What was Liam to do with it all?!

And then another idea struck Liam.

He probably wasn't the only kid
who had ever wanted to get mail.

Dear Mailbox,

Thank you for ALL
the mail! ~~The~~ But I
think it's maybe
too much for just me.
Can you help me send
some of it to other kids?

Love,
        Liam

With some help from the mailbox . . .

. . . Liam was soon mailing things

to kids all over the place!

Liam found he rather liked sending stuff.
He liked it so much that before long,
almost everything was gone.

That was okay with Liam.
He could always ask the
mailbox for more. . . .

But maybe some other time.

FASTER!